Sandy Spade and the Birthday Cake

Written and illustrated
by Andy McGuinness

From the Whistle-On-Sea series

For Archie and Will

Come with me to Whistle-On-Sea...

Every day is special at Whistle-on-Sea. But today was more special than ever. It was Megan's birthday.

Sammy was decorating Beach Hut Bliss when Bertie Bucket and Sandy Spade arrived.

"Hey Sammy, what are you doing so early on the beach?" asked Bertie.

"I'm putting up bunting as a surprise for Megan's birthday," replied Sammy hooking up the colourful flags.

"Oh dear!" said Bertie. "We forgot it was Megan's birthday and we haven't got her a present. What are we going to do?'

"Let's make her a birthday cake," said Sandy.

"Can I help?" came a voice from the skies as Shelby Seagull flew down onto Beach Hut Betty.

"You can, Shelby," said Bertie. "You get the gang together and we'll get the cake mixing ingredients."

"Okeydokey," replied Shelby and off he flew to find his friends.

Sandy suddenly had a thought. "We don't have any cake mix and there's no time to go shopping. That leaves only one thing to make Megan's cake with – sand!"

"Bucket loads of fun!" exclaimed Bertie. "We'll build the best birthday cake ever. You'll help won't you Sammy?"

"Of course I will," Sammy replied. He had finished putting up the bunting and was now hanging up a banner that read 'Happy Birthday'.

"Dig it!" said Sandy. "Megan will be pleased."

A little while later, Shelby had gathered most of the gang together.
There was Kelvin Crab and the Crabettes, Seamus Seaweed, Willie Whelk, Suzy Starfish, Polly Pebble, Marcel Moulé and Larry Lobster.

"Great work Shelby," said Bertie. "Okay everyone, today is Megan's birthday and we're going to make her the best birthday cake ever… out of sand!"

"And we'll decorate it with all sorts of things we find on the beach," added Sandy.

"Let the wild whelk of the west coast get to work," said Willie Whelk excitedly.

Sam had buckets and spades for those who wanted to use them.

"But I'm a superstar," said Suzy Starfish. "I'm not sure I should be digging in the sand."

"You look for things to decorate the cake with," said Seamus Seaweed. "We'll do the digging."

Sammy led everyone to a part of the beach so Megan wouldn't see the cake when she arrived at Beach Hut Betty.

"Let the cake making begin!" he said.
The sand chefs started digging. "Fill me up! Fill me up!" shouted Bertie. Sandy dug deep and filled Bertie to the brim.

"I'm full. Tip me up and pat my bottom," Bertie told his friend.

"This is so much fun!" cried Sandy patting Bertie hard to get all the sand out.

Bertie flipped back the right way up. They had made the perfect sandcastle.

"We don't need sandcastles," said Sammy. "We need a big pile of sand that we can shape into a cake. Like this," he explained shovelling sand into a pile.

Soon a mountain of sand stood in the middle of the beach.

"Now we have to shape it into a cake using our hands and spades," Sam told them.

"Let's not forget the jam and cream," said Larry using his claws to carve the filling.

"He's a sharp one ," said Willie from the top of the cake.

"And what about the icing?"

"Seaweed will make good icing," said Shelby.

"A birthday cake needs candles," shouted Marcel Moulé.

"Leave that to us," came a voice from the other side of the groynes. It was Freddie Flotsam and Jessie Jetsam. They were collecting bundles of driftwood.

"Let's write HAPPY BIRTHDAY in pebbles," suggested Polly Pebble.

"Terrific idea, this is going to be such a great cake," said Bertie beaming with delight.

The gang spent half the morning making Megan's cake. Everyone helped, even Suzy who had scattered shells on the cake to look like sprinkly bits.

"Great teamwork everyone," said Sammy. "Now back to Beach Hut Betty to surprise Megan."

Back at Beach Hut Betty the gang hid inside and waited.

A short while later, they heard footsteps on the decking. It was Megan.

"Where is everyone today?" said Megan to herself.

Suddenly the door of the beach hut burst open.

"We're here!" shouted everyone running out. 'Happy Birthday Megan!" they all cheered, giving her a hug.

"Wow! Thank you so much," said Megan cheerfully." I love what you've done to Betty. What a lovely surprise."

"We have another surprise for you," said Sandy excitedly. "Follow us."

They led Megan to where they had built her birthday cake.

But when they got there they couldn't believe what they saw. Half the cake had gone!

"Oh no!" said Sandy horrified. "The tide has come in and started to eat your birthday cake."

From what was left of the cake, Megan could clearly see how much effort the gang had put into making it.

"You can't blame the sea for eating it, after all, it does look like such a wonderful cake," said Megan.

"We had so much fun making it," sighed Polly.

"Well, it's the thought that counts," said Megan trying to cheer them all up.

"I've got an idea," interrupted Sammy. "Let's all go to the Tea Shack. Birthday cake and ice cream on me!"

"Great!" they all cheered.

"Let's sing a song as we go," suggested Suzy.

"I know a good song," said Kelvin, with a wink to the Crabettes. "Hit it!"

"Happy Birthday to you... Happy Birthday to you... Happy Birthday dear Megan...Happy Birthday to you!"

"What a great birthday this is," said Megan with a big smile.

"It will be even better when Sandy fills me up with that birthday cake," said Bertie.

Everyone laughed.

And skipped.

And sang.

All the way to the Tea Shack for the best birthday tea ever.

The End

Also in the Whistle-On-Sea series…

Bertie Bucket and Sandy Spade are collecting shells to paint on the beach. They find an Oyster Shell, which they hope will contain a pearl. But when an evil seagull called Bagshot kidnaps Bertie and the Oyster Shell, it's left to Shelby Seagull to save the day. Find out how in Bertie Bucket and the Precious Pearl.

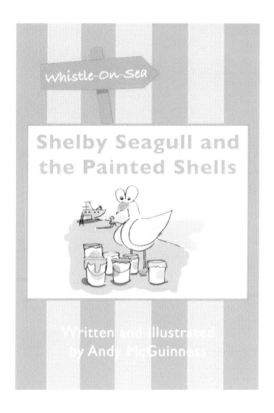

Whistle-On-Sea

Shelby Seagull and
the Painted Shells

Written and Illustrated
by Andy McGuinness

It's a day of painting shells for Megan and the gang, but when the paint runs dry, Shelby Seagull goes in search of fresh supplies. He returns with pots more paint for Larry Lobster and Willie Whelk to splodge and splat on bucket loads of shells. It's only later they discover that what Shelby found was no ordinary paint. Join the fun when Kelvin Crab discovers he has glow-in-the-dark paint on his claws in Shelby Seagull and The Painted Shells.

Whistle-On-Sea

Kelvin Crab and the
Message in a Bottle

Written and Illustrated
by Andy McGuinness

Guitar-playing Kelvin Crab is planning to put on a rock concert at
the Rock Pool, with his band the Crabettes. He decides to send a
message in a bottle to tell all his friends. Realising few people will
see it and not wanting Kelvin to be left feeling disappointed, Megan
and the gang secretly plan other ways to draw the crowds. But will
it work or will the evening be a disaster? Find out in Kelvin Crab
and the Message in a Bottle.

Follow us on Facebook

ABOUT THE AUTHOR

Andy McGuinness has spent his career as an advertising copywriter in London. Inspired by many happy summers spent in Whitstable with his two small boys, he has written the Whistle-On-Sea series.

Printed in Poland
by Amazon Fulfillment
Poland Sp. z o.o., Wrocław